OTHER BOOKS BY
DANIEL KENNEY

The Beef Jerky Gang

Curial Diggs And The Search For The Romanov Dolls

Dart Guns At Dawn

Lunchmeat Lenny 6th Grade Crime Boss

Middle Squad

The Math Inspectors 1

The Math Inspectors 2

The Big Life of Remi Muldoon

Tales Of A Pirate Ninja

Visit DanielKenney.com where parents can sign up to receive

his newsletter and a FREE story.

But I Still Had Feet

Written and illustrated by

DANIEL KENNEY

Rachel ignored the loud knock at the bathroom door and looked in her mouth.

No doubt about it. WIGGLY. Definitely wiggly.

The door rumbled yet again. KNOCK, KNOCK, KNOCK.

Rachel turned to the door. "Go away, Mom, and don't come back. You'll just have to get used to living without a seven year-old daughter, because I am NEVER coming out!"

That's when she heard the laugh. A familiar laugh to be sure, just not the one she was expecting.

"Grandpa?" Rachel asked.

He laughed again. "That's the first time I've been mistaken for your mother."

Rachel growled. So Mom had called Grandpa? Whenever Mom needed backup she always brought in Grandpa. Like he was her secret weapon. That woman would stop at nothing to separate her only daughter from her very wiggly tooth.

"Nice try, Grandpa, but I'm not coming out. Not for Mom and not even for you."

Hmmmmm is all Rachel heard in response. *Oh no,* Grandpa was Hmmmmmming. It was the sound he made whenever he put his hand in his pockets, pushed his lower lip over his upper lip, and rocked back and forth.

It meant he was scheming.

"I just stopped by to tell you something," he finally said.

Fat chance, Rachel thought. "Grandpa, this is a trick and I know it."

"Hmmmmmmmmm," he said again. "I hear you might be losing a tooth."

Rachel stomped her foot. "Is that what Mom told you? Well, I am NOT losing a tooth. My tooth is wiggly, that's all. And my wiggly tooth will be fine and will stay in my mouth for a very long time."

Grandpa chuckled. "Now Rachel, those little teeth have to come out sometime so that your big teeth can come in—that's just the way it works."

Rachel wasn't so sure about that. Had there ever been a scientific study of the teeth losing habits of every one of the billions of people who had ever lived on earth?

"No one is touching my tooth Grandpa!"

"But losing a tooth, especially your first tooth, is a special event. You should be excited."

Okay, that was it. Rachel might love her Grandpa but it was time to set him straight. "Excited? This isn't exciting. This is TERRIBLE! As in the single worst thing that has ever happened to me."

"Well that's disappointing," Grandpa said, "because I really wanted to tell you some great news."

"You'll just have to tell me the news on the other side of that door because I'm not coming out and these teeth will stay locked away safely in my mouth for the rest of my life. And that's that!"

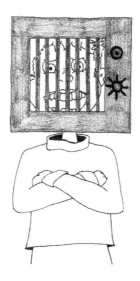

Grandpa let out a big, long sigh. "You know Rachel, I can remember when I was your age and I lost my first tooth. It happened at school and it really wasn't so bad."

Rachel put her finger on the tip of her tooth and wiggled just a bit. She swallowed hard.

"Did it hurt?" she asked.

"Not really," Grandpa said.

"You're lying."

"I am not."

"I bet you remember because it was the most painful experience of your whole life."

"I'm pretty sure listening to your mother practice the violin was the most painful experience of my life. Nope, I remember because, well, to be honest—something very special happened that day."

Rachel thought about what it must feel like to have a tooth yanked out of your mouth. She shivered and turned back to the door. "Something happened?"

"Yep," Grandpa said. "And if you come out of that bathroom, I might just tell you."

Trick. Nothing but a dirty trick. "I'm not coming out," Rachel said.

"Too bad," Grandpa said. "It's really quite a story."

Rachel looked at her wiggly tooth then she looked to the door. It had to be a trick. Right? "I am NOT coming out," she finally said.

"Hmmmmmm," is all Grandpa said from the other side of the door.

A minute or so of silence passed between them until finally Rachel heard shuffling from the other side of the door.

Rachel bit her lip. "Grandpa, do you think you could still tell me the story even if I didn't come out?"

"Hmmmmmm," Grandpa said in reply.

"Please?"

"Well—"

"Maybe, maybe the story will help me, you know, with my tooth?"

"Telling you a story through a door is going to help you with a wiggly tooth that will never, ever come out of your mouth?"

"Please, Grandpa?"

Grandpa let out a loud sigh. "This is very unorthodox."

"But will you do it anyway?" Rachel asked.

There was another long pause, followed by the sound of footsteps, as if Grandpa was walking away. He was leaving? Just like that? When his only granddaughter had a wiggly tooth? How could he?

That's when Rachel heard a THUNK followed by yet another one of her Grandpa's Hmmmms.

"Where did you go?" She asked.

"To get a chair, of course. It's a rather long story and I'm a rather old man. I'd prefer to be comfortable. Now then, I suppose we should start at the beginning."

It was a cold January day and our town had already received, I don't know, around ten feet of snow that winter.

And even with snow piling up all over town, my school had yet to have a day off because our Principal, Mrs. Irene Pomperdash, was not a believer in snow days.

You heard me, not a BELIEVER!

Pomperdash was a tough principal. Being Old School is what *she* called it. Students, Parents, Grizzly Bears—they were all afraid of her.

As a result, the children of our school were well-behaved,

worked hard, and were accustomed to being at school no matter how bad the weather. Like I said, Pomperdash did NOT believe in snow days. And, after our town had already received a hundred feet of snow that winter, things were getting ridiculous.

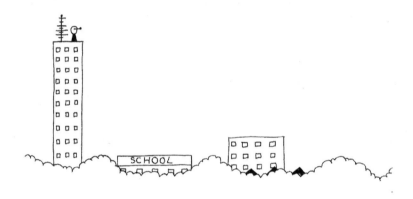

And Pomperdash had been fielding quite a few calls from parents asking when we would finally have a day off. Every other school in town did. But us? NOOOOO. Pomperdash said snow days were for soft kids. She told us one day we'd thank her, and she did not back down.

So, on a very cold, and snow-filled morning, much like today, I was in Mass singing *Joy to the World* when my own very wiggly tooth fell out. I stuck it in my pocket, and when we returned to homeroom, I showed my best friend David. Well, David said I needed to go to the Principal's office and tell Mrs. Pomperdash.

I replied that I'd rather be slowly digested by flesh eating spiders. But David said he was serious.

"You don't understand," David said. "Losing teeth is the one area where Pomperdash has a heart. Word is, she gives out candy."

Well, that did not sound like the Irene Pomperdash I knew but David insisted it was true and that I needed to hustle up to her office so I could score myself a lollipop.

I thought there was a very good chance David was just trying to get me beaten up but the possibility of candy was too alluring to turn down. So I did it. I marched up to the Principal's office, knocked twice, and she threw the door open so hard I thought it might come off it's hinges.

She folded her arms and started to breathe in and out real heavy—like she was trying to suck up tiny bits of my soul. My body shook so hard I thought I might shatter into a thousand pieces. She asked what I needed and though I didn't have the courage to form words, I managed to open my mouth. That's when she relaxed.

Slightly.

"So, you lost a tooth?" Pomperdash asked.

I nodded.

"Let me see it then," she said as she extended her hand palm facing up. I handed over the tooth and she began inspecting it at once.

Finally, she looked up and nodded. "This does indeed appear to be a genuine child's tooth. You can choose a piece of candy from the jar."

I looked over behind her desk at this big beautiful jar filled with candy.

So it really WAS TRUE.

"Or," Pomperdash said, her eyes twinkling and her finger at her chin.

"Or what?" I asked.

"Or, you could choose from the surprise box?"

"The surprise box?"

She pointed to an old wooden box on the opposite side of her office. It looked like a briefcase but made from wood with old rusty hinges.

"What's in the surprise box?" I asked.

"You have to choose it to find out."

A long moment passed as I thought about my options. Go for the candy jar and get a sure thing OR choose the surprise box and possibly get nothing. That's the kind of psycho Irene Pomperdash was. She'd put nothing in a surprise box just to see you cry.

"You're wasting my time," Pomperdash said as she TAP,

TAP, TAPPED her fingers against her desk.

Truth was, as much as I wanted that candy, I wanted to know what kind of things Pomperdash might have in a surprise box even more. I walked over to the old wooden box and opened it up.

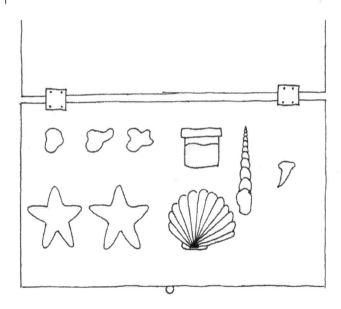

Inside were the kinds of objects that I was NOT expecting. Polished rocks, a small jar of sand, a couple silver dollar star fish, a sea shell and, on the far right of the surprise box, something else. Something far cooler than everything else.

I looked up at Pomperdash. "Is this a shark's tooth?"

She narrowed her eyes. "A baby shark's tooth, to be precise. Now make a choice, I've got a school to run."

I couldn't believe Pomperdash had a shark's tooth. It was seriously cool, about the size of the tooth I'd just lost, and sharp. Not razor sharp, mind you, but sharp enough to cut if you weren't careful.

So, I took that shark's tooth in one hand and Mrs. Pomperdash took my other hand, crushed it in her vice-like grip, and wished me a good day. But before I left, I stopped and asked if she thought we'd ever get a snow day.

Pomperdash laughed the kind of laugh that witches laugh in the movies. Then she slammed the door in my face.

I walked back to class and showed David my prize. He thought it was so cool that he started wiggling his teeth back and forth and that's when he came up with the bright idea to see what it would look like if I stuck that shark tooth where my old tooth used to be.

Well, since I was a knucklehead seven year-old boy, that's exactly what I did. I stuck that baby shark tooth right in the little pocket where my old tooth had been and you know what, that shark tooth was a perfect fit.

So perfect that it stuck in there without me having to hold it. Kinda like it was almost meant to be there.

So there I was with that shark tooth in my mouth, grinning

at my buddy David and at first he's grinning back and then slowly the expression on his face starts to change, and not in a good way.

"What's wrong David?" I asked but all he could do is point at me and mumble something incoherent.

David looked like he had seen a ghost and that's when I noticed my head. It felt funny. Really funny. Like a pillow suddenly got stuffed inside my brain.

David's expression went all psycho and he screamed.

Then someone else screamed. I tried to turn my head but it felt so big and heavy that it was difficult to move. In fact I now realized that I was the one who didn't feel so good. And then I heard more screams and then I jumped out of my seat and then even more screams and that's when I looked down at my hands.

Well, not hands exactly.

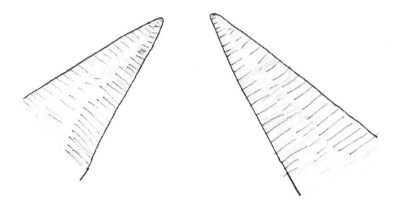

I looked down at my dorsal fins. That's right granddaughter, my head felt funny, my hands were gone, and I had dorsal fins.

DORSAL FINS!

Fish fins. Big fish fins. Bluish grey in color and I'm not sure you know this but dorsal fins are quite hard to move. Not nearly as useful as hands. Anyways, as soon as I realized it I screamed. Or rather, I tried to scream but instead the only thing that came out was: ROARTHUMPMAGOO.

Well, I learned something pretty important that day. One should not ROARTHUMPMAGOO in a room full of kids. Because, as soon as you could say Jack Robinson, the kids in my class all screamed and ran out of the classroom while I stayed back ROARTHUMPMAGOOING to myself, trying to figure out what might have happened. And that's when I saw it, my reflection. Staring back at me from the full length mirror that hung next to our teacher's desk.

I had an enormous blue grey head. Gills. Snout. Sharp teeth.

Dorsal fins. Long body. Yep, there was no doubt about it.

I WAS A SHARK.

And a big one at that. In fact, a much bigger shark than I would've figured I'd be if I had ever considered how big I would be if I were to one day become a shark. I was a big grey shark with teeth that would frighten a T-Rex. Two minutes earlier, I was a regular boy and then boom, like that, I was all shark. Well, almost.

Strange as it sounds—although I had turned into a shark,

I STILL HAD FEET.

That's right, feet. Regular boy feet, tucked inside fancy

sneakers. Weird huh? Well, I didn't have time to reflect on the

weirdness of it all. I was so scared by the shark I saw in that

mirror that I ran out of the classroom and down the hall, like I

was running from something big and scary. But ahead of me, all

the kids in the school were running down the hall, and I supposed it didn't even occur to me that those kids might just be running from me.

And that's when I fell down. Just fell down like a big clump in the middle of the hallway. My first thought was that I had tripped since sharks aren't probably used to having feet but as I lay on the floor gasping for breath—it hit me. It wasn't my feet, it was my GILLS.

And it wasn't that my gills were broken. Far as I could tell they were working exactly the way gills were supposed to work. THAT was the problem. Gills take oxygen out of water and at the moment, all I was sucking in was a bunch of air. My poor

shark body just flat gave out before it even had a chance.

So there I was laying on that cold tile, gasping for oxygen. I

felt kids crowding in on me and that's when I heard one voice

stand out above the crowd.

My best bud David.

He was telling everybody I needed water and he was right.

That was it exactly. WATER. As soon as he said it I didn't

think I'd ever wanted anything so badly in all my life. I tried to

agree with him by saying yes but all that happened was my mouth

opened, I ROARTHUMPMAGOOED, and everybody jumped

back, on account of them thinking I was about to eat them. I

couldn't blame them since I somehow managed to take a big bite

out of Ryan Dingle's pants.

Anyways, David grabbed a water bottle, filled it up at the closest water fountain and dumped it over my gills. And for a moment it felt so good. Like the way cotton candy tastes when you take that very first bite.

But it wasn't enough water. Not even close. I went back to wheezing and gasping for oxygen and that's when I heard the voice of Principal Pomperdash. Got to hand it to her, scary situations call for scary people and she took charge immediately.

"This shark needs to be in water, now!" Pomperdash said it

like I was just one of many sharks she'd encountered face down

on the hallway tile of her school through the years. She ordered

all the kids around me to grab hold and they started dragging

me down the hall. I was gasping and wheezing the whole time and

the cold tile of the school felt like ice on my skin. And then I

realized where they were taking me. To the school's indoor pool.

They plopped me into the school's pool and for a bit I thought

everything was better. I was breathing, my skin felt alive and I

figured I'd be okay. Well, accept for the fact that I WAS

STILL A SHARK. But then, something started burning

and I began to twitch. Right there in the middle of that pool I started to violently twitch. Something else was wrong. Very wrong. I stuck my face out of that water and there was Mrs. Pomperdash, taking control again. She was pointing at me and that's when she smacked her fist into her hand and yelled: "IT'S NOT SALT WATER!"

I hadn't even thought of that. Of course, sharks live in salt water. They NEED salt water. Right about then, everything started to go fuzzy for me. Probably the lack of oxygen combined with the lack of salt water, and before I knew it, my head felt impossibly heavy and everything went black.

When I woke up, I was high above the sky, strapped

into a harness, dangling from a rope which was attached to a

helicopter.

I put two and two together which surprised me because I

wasn't at all certain that Sharks could do math. Pomperdash

must have figured the only way to save me was to fly me to

the ocean as quickly as possible. Now, I gotta be honest, you

might think turning into a shark is pretty scary but that's

nothing compared to dangling from a helicopter a couple

thousand feet above the ground.

The lack of water, the lack of salt, the air hitting my eyeballs, the general sense of terror, well, I didn't think things could get much worse.

I heard something.

COUGH. SPUTTER. SPLURGH!

Overhead the helicopter started to heave back and forth.

Something was wrong. Something was very wrong.

And then, things got much wronger.

You heard me. WRONGER!

I started to fall.

Those blasted helicopter guys cut me loose—apparently more concerned with their own hides than a big shark with feet. But I didn't have time to be bitter. I had more important things to worry about. Like that little thing called the earth's surface which was threatening to squash me like a bug.

But one look down was enough to give me hope. All I saw was blue. Those blasted helicopter guys at least had the decency to cut me loose above the ocean. A memory came to me, of Johnny Edmond's birthday party and the hope didn't last. I got pushed off the high dive by Sheila Dinklage at that party and did a belly flop. That hurt sooooo much and that was only twelve feet above the water. Currently, I was like a THOUSAND FEET above the water. Belly flopping against the surface of the ocean after falling from a thousand feet was not something I wanted to do and I didn't have much time to think.

So....

I DECIDED TO DIVE.

I figured the only chance I had was to hit that water the way those divers do in the Olympics, with no splash. I pointed my head down and tried to keep myself as straight and pointy as a missile.

I braced myself, closed my eyes, shut my big shark mouth tight, and prayed. I'm guessing I was the first praying shark in history.

Those Olympic divers would have been proud. I hit the water perfectly. No splash. At least, I think there was no splash. I just knew that I was alive. But, in hindsight, I may have hit the water a little too perfectly.

You see, the water didn't slow me down. Not one bit. I kept going. Like I was a high speed drill bit boring through Jell-O.

Apparently, you build up quite a bit of speed when you're dropped from a couple thousand feet.

But part of me didn't care. I was in water again, and this time, the right kind of water. SALT WATER. My gills felt great and the very tips of my shark body sprang to life. And I must have been so thankful that I didn't really pay attention to where I was headed.

It was a hole in the ocean floor. Now, technically, I think you'd call it a hydrothermal vent but of course I didn't know it at the time. To me, it was a big hole and I couldn't slow down or change directions.

THOOOOOMP!

I hit that hydrothermal vent at the bottom of the ocean and kept right on going: just rocketing down this hole, still full of water, but water that was increasingly growing hot. And, next thing I knew, the water wasn't just hot, it was steaming, and then THOOOMP THOOMP I felt like I was actually getting sucked down that tunnel; like I'd gotten stuck in a giant vacuum tube that was taking me on a journey to the center of the earth. Along the way, I experienced the most nausea inducing pain I'd ever experienced in my life and then, I hit something hard, stopped moving, and the pain mostly stopped.

I was staring up at some kind of cave. Large stalactites pointed down, like large spikes ready to drop on my head. And suddenly, I had the feeling that I was being watched. I sat up.

Strange, round creatures stared back at me. They had tiny

little stumps for arms, stumps for legs, and tiny wisps of hair.

But for the most part, they were just round little balls, grey and

light brown in color.

I stumbled to my feet and then realized I was much bigger

than these creatures. They must have realized it too because

they stepped back and let out a collective gasp.

One of the round guys pointed his stubby little arm at me,

furrowed his brow and started walking towards me. Then he stopped,

covered his mouth with both of his arms and yelled: "WOOGANDO!"

"WOOGANDO?" the little round creatures all said in reply.

The creature out front arched one eyebrow and rubbed his stubby little arm across his face. "I am certain of it. The great WOOGANDO has finally come. We are SAVED!"

"WE ARE SAVED!" the crowd of round creatures yelled.

I opened up my mouth to speak but then I remembered that all I would probably say would be ROARTHUMPMAGOO. But, to my surprise, I didn't ROARTHUMPMAGOO at all.

I spoke. Words. Wordy words.

"I don't know what you're talking about," I said. "I don't know any WOOGANDO. I'm a boy. A seven year-old boy named Eddie."

The creature up front was confused. He looked back at the crowd, then shrugged and turned to me.

"You are a seven year-old boy named Eddie? Are you sure, because you look more like a Woogando to me."

"Well, I mean, I was a boy until I turned into a shark."

The creature's eyes lit up and he bounced up and down on his stubby legs. He pointed at me. "SHARK, SHARK, SHARK. Yes indeed. WOOGANDO. SHARK."

"Woodgando is your word for Shark?"

He nodded. "My name is BooHooHoo, I am Grand Leader of the Mopes."

"What on earth is a Mope?" I asked.

He was instantly offended.

"The correct question is what under the earth is a Mope," he said. Then he stepped to the side and motioned with his arm. At once, the little round creatures began to bounce up and down on their stumps, then chanted: MOPES, MOPES, MOPES!

"Ohhh," I finally said. "That's what kind of creatures you are. You're Mopes."

"And I'm Grand Leader of the Mopes. This is my second in command, SissyPants. And our number three is RunsAwayCrying.

"And you are Woogando and you are here to save us."

"No," I said. "I came here quite by accident. Long and confusing story but all I really want to do is find a way back to my home in Illinois."

"Ahhhhh," BooHooHoo said. "We will help you back to your home, just after you save us, Great Woogando."

I was seriously confused, but also intrigued. "And how exactly will I save you? I've never saved anybody before."

BooHooHoo bounced up on his little stumps. "Very simple, you will lead us into battle against the Zeds, our fearsome enemy. You will destroy them and make them weep and regret that they ever deal sadness to us Mopes. There will be a terrible wailing and gnashing of teeth throughout the land of the Zeds because of you, O GREAT WOOGANDO."

This all sounded very intense. And scary. And painful.

"You want me to go into battle? I've never been in a battle before and I don't really like the sound of it very much. When is this battle supposed to occur?"

"The battle is right now and you are in the middle of it."

It was at that moment that I felt I was being watched by somebody else. I slowly turned.

Thirty feet away, a crowd of pointy creatures stared at me. The one in front was quite large, had scary eyes, and showed his teeth. I felt BooHooHoo waddle up beside me. I looked down.

"Who are they?" I asked.

"They are the Zeds, of course," He said. "They and their pointy heads have held us Mopes down for far too long. The Head Zed is a ruthless man named Ned. But that was in the past. With your help, Great Woogando, today the MOPES STRIKE BACK!"

Ned stepped towards me. "Yes," he snarled, "I am the head Zed Ned and my job is to make Mopes dead."

At that, the Zeds behind Ned laughed like Ned had just said the funniest thing in the world. And I have to admit, I became angry. Even though I was a boy who had turned into a shark, at the moment, I felt very much like a Mope and I was rather tired of this Head Zed dope.

"I don't like this Ned very much," I said to BooHooHoo.

"Of course not, you are Woogando, and you have been brought here to save us."

"But, you don't understand, I've never been in a battle before."

"NO worries, you are Woogando. You have little Zeds inside your mouth. Any creatures that has Zeds inside his mouth will have no problem destroying the Zeds for us."

I gulped a very large Woogando gulp.

"I can hear you talking BooHooHoo," said the head Zed Ned as he walked closer. "I don't care how large this thing is or how many Zeds he has in his mouth. Us Zeds will destroy you today just like we always do and I will dance on this Woogando's cold lifeless corpse.

"I have to be honest," I told BooHooHoo, "I don't like the sound of this at all. By the way, how exactly do the Zeds always defeat you in battle?"

"Are you kidding me?" BooHooHoo replied. "The Zeds are pointy and we are not. All we can do is throw rocks and run into them while they just POKE, POKE, POKE at us with their pointy Zed heads." He let out a sigh. "I dread those Zed Heads."

"But I don't want any Mopes to get hurt," I said.

"Good, that's what I was hoping you would say." BooHooHoo stepped forward towards Ned, bowed deeply and then raised his arms to the air. "The Great Woogando challenges Ned the Head Zed to a Duel to the Dead."

I also didn't like the sound of that and was instantly filled with dread.

Zed shrieked and jumped in the air. "HA, HA, HA! You dare to challenge Ned to a duel to the dead? What has gone wrong in your round, mush-filled head?"

I was scared and growing dizzy from all the bad rhyming.

BooHooHoo pushed me closer to Ned. Ned snarled at me and chomped on his teeth. If I had looked at the situation rationally, I shouldn't have been so scared. Zed was a triangle and I was a shark. He had a pointy head and I had a big mouth with sharp teeth.

But Ned the Head Zed had been in battles and had made Mopes Dead. And I was scared of his sharp pointy head. I could hardly move, my feet felt like lead.

"I will enjoy defeating you strange creature," Ned said. "I will stick the pointy end of my head in your weird creature shaped body. When I am done, you will be dead. Then, the Zeds will have gained their greatest victory yet."

I looked to BooHooHoo. "What's he talking about?"

"If you lose the Duel to the Dead, it will be our final defeat. Us Mopes will retire to the Gizzard of Gorgongola where we will live out our days in misery."

"What is the Gizzard of Gorgongola?" I asked.

All BooHooHoo could do was shake his Mopey head and make a very sour face.

He finally looked at me with sadness in his eyes. "Help us, Great Woogando, you're our only hope."

I gulped again. BooHooHoo had quoted Princess Leia. Even though he had never seen Star Wars, *he had quoted Princess Leia.* Which meant, I was his Obi One Kanobi. Which meant, I was a Jedi.

Whoa.

Ned snarled and snapped his teeth. "Prepare to die, strange

creature."

I realized I did not have a light saber. Maybe I could try something else.

"I am not the droid you're looking for," I said as I waved my dorsal fin across my face.

Zed roared. "You dare to insult my mother Droid Zed? Prepare for death!!!!"

Okay, I was definitely not a Jedi and come on, what were the odds his mother's name was Droid? Zed crouched low and lowered the sharp point of his head towards me. My shark body started to shake. I was in big trouble. I was in a duel to the dead with an experienced combat veteran who thought I just insulted his mother. I needed a way out of this. I went with the first thing that came to me.

I put one dorsal fin over the other. "Time out," I yelled.

Zed straighted up. "Time out?"

"Yes, a timeout. You have angered me greatly. Ned and therefore a duel to the dead is not a large enough price for your head. I propose a different duel instead."

"This is unprecedented," Zed said to BooHooHoo. "Who does this strange creature think he is? According to the Second Equilateral Council, once the Duel has commenced there is no stopping."

BooHooHoo gave me a weird look.

"Trust me," I said. "Ahhh, and that is all you remember because you, Ned, are dumb and are the leader of a notoriously stupid group of creatures. There is a reason your heads are so pointy. Because your brain is so little."

"What does that mean?" asked Ned.

"It means that you forget about the Isosceles Papers, both the Third and Fourth Volumes."

Ned put both stubby hands on his hips. His mouth twisted in confusion. "The Isosceles Papers?"

"Of for the love of Zed," I said. "According to the Isosceles Papers, a participant can raise the Duel of the Dead at any moment to the far more important Duel of the Dance."

"Duel of the Dance?"

"Yes, instead of killing each other, we dance. Whoever Dances better, wins. Loser spends his days in the Gizzard of Gorgongola."

"You want to Dance against me?" Zed said.

"Yes, unless you're too scared."

"Scared? HA! The only thing Zed is better at than fighting is dancing."

"Really?" I said.

BooHooHoo had his face in his hands.

"Really?" I said again.

"Oh yes," BooHooHoo said. "Ned's dancing is legendary. You have sealed our fate. It is no use. I will go prepare the Mopes for the journey to Gorgongola."

"Enough stalling," Zed said. "The Duel of the Dance starts now." Zed jumped into the air and spun. Then he pranced to one side, then the other. He was doing ballet. BALLET. And he was...unbelievable. I watched for the next minute in horror as Zed jumped, twisted, and danced like he was a world famous ballet dancer.

And I knew I had made a gigantic mistake.

When he finished, he bowed deeply and then he popped up and pointed at me. "Time to go down strange creature!"

But I wasn't about to back down. I pointed back.

"No it isn't," I said.

I would really need to work on my snappy comebacks. "Wait a second," I said. "I can't dance without music. And according to the Isosceles papers, if music is not provided, then both sides agree to a rematch in exactly one year."

"A year?" said Zed.

"A year," I said. "Even longer if chunky peanut butter can't be located."

I saw the look on Zed's face. I might have finally flummoxed the overgrown triangle.

Just then I heard music. I turned around. My heart sunk.

It appeared that Sissy Pants had miraculously come up with a boom box. Looked like I was all out of excuses. I closed my eyes and tried to remember all the dance moves I'd seen my dad do while washing dishes and trying to annoy my mom. I took a deep breath and began.

I started off with the Cowboy, then transitioned into Horseback Gangham style. Then I threw out Jazz fins and it occurred to me that Jazz Fins look a lot like the letter Y. Which meant, I was going right into the YMCA. I was now on a roll. I Hokey Pokeyed, Limboed, and pulled out the Cuetip. And it was time for my big finish.

I pulled out the Fishing Pole and finished strong, throwing

down disco Saturday Night Fever style.

When I couldn't dance anymore, I fell into a heap onto the cave floor. I'd done everything I could do and I hoped somewhere my dad and his overbite would be proud. Sissy Pants turned off the music. When I looked up, the whole place was silent. Then Ned the head Zed fell to his knees, buried his head and screamed out in anguish. NOOOOOOOOO!

Behind me the Mopes screamed. I jumped up, pumped my dorsal fins in victory and was mobbed by Mopes. It was easily the greatest moment of my short shark life.

The Mopes carried me off the field of battle chanting WOOGANDO, WOOGANDO, WOOGANDO!

I turned and saw BooHooHoo smiling, a little tear running down his fat Mopey cheek. "You saved us Woogando, you really saved us. And to reward you, we are giving you the King's Bath before we send you home."

I had to be honest. I needed a bath. I didn't really understand why I was able to get oxygen from this strange underground world while not immersed in water but I also didn't understand why these creatures were able to understand my words nor why I had turned into a shark in the first place!

I was operating in unfamiliar territory. That being said, getting back into water sounded like heaven. And a King's Bath? I mean, being a shark wasn't my favorite thing in the world, but a King's Bath sounded pretty darn nice.

Unfortunately, the Mopes' idea of a hero's reward was quite a bit different than mine. Turns out, the King's Bath wasn't filled with water at all. By the looks of the orange bubbly liquid and the feel of the insane heat, I was pretty sure the King's Bath was filled with molten lava.

You heard me. LAVA.

When I pointed this out to BooHooHoo, he sighed and said that yes, he wished he could also take the King's Bath but only one of us was the real hero. That's when he yelled: FOR THE GREAT WOOGANDO and the crowd of Mopes threw me into the air. I flapped my dorsal fins in hopes I might learn to fly but it was too late. I hit the lava, felt pain like I'd never felt before in my life and then—well, nothing.

In case you didn't know, a Shark cannot float in lava. Furthermore, a Shark cannot live in lava. Far as I can tell, the only think that CAN float in lava or live in lava is lava.

After hitting that lava, my poor shark body went POOF and completely disintegrated. Yet, somehow I can't explain, I was still alive. The whole thing was preposterous. There I was, a Particularly Preposterous Pile of lava bubbling away in a Precarious Plethora of magma soup. That's when I heard the noise, as if the earth was the belly of an enormous beast groaning for life. Then the groaning stopped and things grew calm.

Too calm.

With a BOOOOOM, WHOOSH, BWURRRRPLOOK, I was launched straight up so fast I thought my stomach was dropping into my belly which was weird since I was just a pile of lava and didn't have a stomach or a belly.

I shot up through a volcano and high into the air. And—as I and a bunch of other lava shot into the air—something happened. The wind and the clouds caught us and suddenly I noticed that I was surrounded by nothing but a bunch of hot gray ash. Well, I knew if all the other lava had turned into ash, then that's what must have happened to me. I was a big cloud of ash being driven by a strong, mighty wind moving awfully fast.

When. I was a shark, dangling high in the air from that helicopter, bouncing along, that was scary. But being grey ash blown by a terrific wind high above the tallest clouds? Well, that wasn't scary at all.

IT WAS GLORIOUS.

I settled into a calm and blew lazily right along. I can't tell you how long I floated in that wind. Being a clump of volcanic ash I'm fairly certain I didn't have a brain and not having a brain makes you sort of confused.

So, at some point I found myself falling slowly and steadily to the earth until I landed gently on the ground. There I was, volcanic ash surrounded by more volcanic ash. The whole thing felt cuddly, like a big pillow, and then I drifted off to sleep.

At least I think I fell asleep. Again, the whole not having a brain thing was discombobulating. Well, asleep or not, the next thing I remember was moving again, being turned upside down, spun back right side up and finally settling down.

I looked out. Then I looked next to me. I was still volcanic ash but now I was in a glass jar. I was surrounded by other glass jars of volcanic ash. I was in some sort of a store. Well, again I'm not sure how the thought occurred to me since I didn't have a brain, but the thought DID occur to me that I was in trouble. Then I noticed something—that even though I was volcanic ash, stuck inside of a sealed glass jar, I could definitely feel that underneath the rest of me,

I STILL HAD FEET

I giggled. I mean, WHAT ON EARTH WAS GOING ON? I was supposed to be a seven year-old boy but instead I was a jar of volcanic ash with feet. That's when I stopped giggling. Because truth be told, I wasn't happy. Not at all. I was mad. I needed to get home. I needed to find a way to stop being volcanic ash. And, like I said, thankfully I STILL HAD FEET!

I bounced up and down in my jar. I moved my feet side to side and pretty soon, I had that jar rocking back and forth. I was hitting the glass jars of volcanic ash right next to me. Rocking back and forth, back and forth, back and forth. And then, I fell. I toppled over the edge of the shelf, landed on the floor and when I did, I felt something crack along the bottom. I stomped my feet straight down and managed to kick out two holes just big enough for my feet to get through.

I ran through that store, dodging shoppers as they strolled merrily along, completely unaware that a seven year-old former shark of a boy was now confined to a glass jar as little more than grey ash with feet. And finally, when the door to the store opened, I bolted outside.

Wow, what a beautiful day! The sun's rays felt warm on, well, I suppose I didn't have skin. So, the sun just felt warm. And there I was, a jar of volcanic ash wandering outside, under a warm sun, for the moment trying to forget the predicament I was in.

But I remembered in a hurry. As soon as I heard the ROARRRRRR of an engine. I looked up and saw a car coming right toward me.

I turned and ran. Problem was, I was a tiny jar of volcanic ash with even tinier feet and I couldn't run very fast and just barely made it to the grass when I heard and felt the WHOOSH of the car as it just missed crushing me. I kept running further into the grass and when I was certain I was safe, I stopped and looked up.

And as I looked up, I saw something else that was very large. But this very large thing was not a car and at the moment was busy chewing on some grass.

It was a BUFFALO!

Holy Cow, err, Holy Buffalo. Next to rhinos, buffaloes were my favorite animals in the world and I'd never seen one in person let along this close. Well, this is where the not having a brain thing really hurt me. I walked closer to that buffalo for a better look. The buffalo stopped chewing. Then he eyed me. Then he stomped his foot against the ground and snot bubbled out of his enormous nostrils.

The ground rumbled and coming up alongside this large

buffalo were other very large buffaloes.

And I was starting to get a very bad feeling about all of this.

"Nice buffalo," I said as I began to slowly walk backwards. And then I felt more rumbling as several buffaloes kicked their hooves against the ground, and bubbled snot from their noses.

Bit of advice Granddaughter, if you ever find yourself in this position, foot stomping and snot bubbling are all signs to turn around and

RUNNNNNNNNNN!!!!!!

As I ran, the ground shook like an earthquake, the animals roared and it felt like their hot breath was right behind me. I thought I was a goner for sure.

And then another in what had become a long list of very strange things happened.

I heard a different noise, like a shriek, the air around me shook, something snatched my foot, and I was suddenly upside down and being lifted quickly into the air.

Part of me was terrified, but I was also quite glad that I'd been saved from that herd of buffalo. So I thought the proper thing was to thank my hero.

"Thank you kind sir," I said as I dangled from the air.

"You won't thank me for long," came a low voice. "I wasn't saving you, I was HUNTING you."

Hunting me? Wait a second. I tried to crane my neck and then I remembered I not only didn't have a brain, I probably also didn't have a neck.

"Um, excuse me, what exactly are you?"

"I'm an owl," my hero responded.

An owl? *Now, that was something.* I noticed the sun continuing to pour it's warmth out onto the day, and something occurred to me. "I thought owls were nocturnal—that means they hunt at night."

"You are a very clever little thing aren't you?" answered the owl. "And of course owls are nocturnal and of course I would know that since I am an owl."

"Then why are you hunting me during the day?" I asked. "Maybe you forgot it was day and it would be better to set me down safely in some nice comfortable car traveling to Illinois?"

The owl hooted. "You're clever AND you're funny. I will regret having to eat you. No, clever funny little thing, I am an ambitious owl and one night it occurred to me that us owls are missing out on an extraordinary market opportunity. One that I intended to exploit. As long as the other owls were going to sleep during the day, I figured that was the perfect time for me to swoop in and hunt up all the food."

"I have to be honest, that sounds like cheating?"

"Cheating?" said the owl.

"Yes," I said. "Cheating. How is it fair competition if the other owls don't even know you're doing this?"

"You must be a communist," answered the owl in a disapproving voice. "Capitalism my boy, pure economic Darwinism. If the other owls aren't clever enough to spot this opportunity then they certainly don't deserve—"

THUMPPPPP

Something hit us hard, the owl screamed, and I was ripped free of the owl and flown in a different direction. This time, I managed to spot the WHO who had me.

"You're a hawk!" I said.

"You're talking?" the hawk said as he looked at me. "Usually when I crush a vermin's throat, he can't breathe let along talk."

"See, that's the problem, you don't have me by the throat, you've got me by the leg," I said.

The hawk squawked. "That explains it. Would you mind

showing me where your throat is so I could crush it, end you're life, and have a peaceful flight back to my nest."

"I'm afraid not," I said.

"You dare to refuse ME, a hawk?"

"The thing is," I said. "I'm not sure I have a throat."

"Don't have a throat? What kind of madness is this? What kind of rodent are you anyway? A squirrel, right? That's got to be it, you're the world's ugliest squirrel."

"Nope. I'm volcanic ash, trapped inside a glass jar. Oh, and I have feet."

"And tiny little legs."

"You're right, feet *and* legs. Near as I can tell, I don't have any internal organs. Just a bunch of very unappetizing ash."

The hawk shook me like he was mad. "There you go again with that word, ASH. I'm not familiar with ash. Does it taste like chicken?"

"It tastes like dirt, you won't like ash one bit. Better to set me down in some nice comfortable car on its way to Illinois."

"I knew it," said the Hawk, "this is a trick. Are you a nice tasty rabbit pretending to be this ASH?"

"No sir Mr. Hawk."

"Well, don't you worry. I know we can eat your legs and your feet and the rest? It will make a nice garnishment with our meal. My wife keeps telling me I need more fiber in my diet."

This hawk was determined and I needed to outwit him. "No, I promise, I'm ten times less tasty than dirt. And, I'd give you a terrible stomach ache."

"Ha, now I know it's a trick. There's only one animal that gives Hawks stomach aches. Dogs."

"DOGS!" I screamed. "You eat dogs?"

"You're not listening, of course I don't eat dogs. They give you terrible tummy aches. Us raptors call it a leaky gut. You can be assured that I never ever eat dogs. There's only two rules when you're a hawk. First, don't eat dogs. Second, never hunt around eagles."

"Why?" I asked.

"Well, as embarrassing as it is to admit, eagles are bigger, tougher, and according to the girls, better looking. And they like to bully us hawks."

"I'm sorry."

"Don't be, I'm about to rip your feet off your legs and feed the rest of you to my children. Don't cry for this hawk."

"No, I mean, I'm sorry you don't see that eagle coming right at us."

"WHATTT!" the hawk screamed.

THUMPPP!!!

That big eagle whacked Mr. Hawk in the rump feathers and grabbed my other leg all in one violent motion. The hawk fell below us and the eagle quickly carried me much higher into the air.

"So you're an eagle." I said it almost like an accusation.

"Hey, hey, hey," came a raspy voice. "How'd you know?"

"Because I know what eagles look like and because Mr. Hawk back there was saying how hawks are scared of eagles and then WHACK! Just like that, you grabbed me."

"Hey, hey, hey," the eagle said again. We kept rising, further and further into the sky."

"Um, Mr. Eagle, you might be curious to know that I'm a dog

and am responsible for leaky gut syndrome in raptor birds all over the world."

"Ha!" said the Eagle. "So Mr. Hawk told you about Leaky Gut, did he? Well, strange animal in my grasp who is definitely NOT a dog. I am an Eagle and I have a cast iron stomach. I once ate a jeep without hardly a burp. I am not a weenie like the hawk. I've known dogs, I've worked with dogs, I've eaten dogs, and you, Sir, are no dog."

"I don't suppose you'd believe I'm a jar of thumbtacks or a bottle of poison?"

"No I would not. Fact is, you're going to be eaten. I don't even care if you taste good. I don't care if you're difficult to eat. Makes no difference to me. I'm an eagle, king of the sky, and I got a reputation to protect. I stole you from that hawk and I darn well plan on eating you. In fact, the only thing that could possibly keep me from eating you would be—"

THUMPPPPPP!

We were hit impossibly hard by something impossibly large. The eagle turned into a cloud of black and white feathers and I was hurled upward further at a ridiculously fast rate. That's right. We were hit by an **AIRPLANE!**

"STOPPPPPP GRANDPA!" yelled Rachel. "Are you saying that the eagle died?"

Well, I can't say for sure but one moment he was talking to me and the next he was a cloud of feathers that didn't talk so that was my assumption.

"But that's horrible!"

I suppose it is but you must remember, this eagle was about to eat me and, being at the top of the food chain, had eaten countless other animals plus a very innocent jeep on one occasion. I wouldn't feel too bad for that eagle, nor did I since at the moment I was a jar of volcanic ash hurtling further and further into the sky.

"What happened?"

I'll tell you what happened, you interrupted me in the middle of my story.

"No, Grandpa, what happened next?"

Well, I don't know if it was the collision with that airplane or the freezing cold air but I began to feel the glass in that jar go CRACK and before you knew it...that jar exploded into pieces.

Up I blew, further and further into the freezing cold atmosphere, I blew, no longer comfortable mind you. Nope, air this cold was definitely NOT comfortable and I was getting lost in the fog of the clouds and suddenly I felt very different. No longer cold even though I could tell I was surrounded by something very, very white and was once again falling back to the ground.

I had turned into SNOW!

So there I was again, falling down to earth and this time not as volcanic ash but as white fluffy snow. But whereas I was very out of it falling to the ground as ash, as snow, I knew exactly what was going on. I saw something below me.

Something familiar.

MY TOWN!

By some miracle, I must have gotten swept up into the jet stream and been brought back to my hometown in Illinois. And, as I watched my town come into focus, I noticed one thing in particular. A thousand feet of snow sure has a way of piling up.

And to think, Pomperdash HAD NOT given us even one snow day.

So I continued to fall lazily through the cold winter sky and the buildings and landmarks of my town grew larger as I came closer to the ground. And that's when I noticed I wasn't just falling to my town, I was falling to my SCHOOL!

What luck!

The parking lot was filling up, which could mean only one thing, it was the end of the day. After everything I'd been through, this really was lucky.

And I remembered, I was just a bunch of snow. That wasn't lucky at all. Not one bit.

Suddenly I grew very sad and trust me, the world does not need sad snowflakes.

I know what you're thinking, I should have been more thankful. Thankful about the fact that despite turning into a shark, almost falling to my death, turning into molten lava, shooting out of a volcano, blowing across the country and now falling back down to earth as snow—that despite all of it, I was still alive. But what can I say? I was a seven year-old boy at heart and I really wanted a snow day.

And I was so preoccupied with being a sad snowflake, that I didn't even realize I was close to the ground until I landed with a soft PLOP. I looked around and all I could see were feet and all I could hear were voices. The reasonably happy voices of kids leaving school for the day.

Then I heard a particular voice. One that was not reasonably happy and that stood out among all the rest. The hard edged voice of....

IRENE POMPERDASH.

It was Principal Pomperdash and she was speaking to someone. "Of course we won't have a snow day," she shrieked.

"No, I don't care how much more snow we get. You'll thank me when you're older and you realize it was Irene Pomperdash who taught you how to survive in a tough and unforgiving world."

I don't know why, but that set me off. And if I would have been a boy instead a clump of snow, I would have screamed or thrown my backpack. After all I had been through, Pomperdash somehow believed NOT giving snow days is what makes students ready for the world?

UNBELIEVABLE.

Pomperdash kept talking and I could hear her voice growing louder. I looked up and could finally see her. Coming right behind me.

I had an idea. I made a decision. And I did something I'm not particularly proud of. And when it was done, Pomperdash went flying through the air and fell face first into a large drift of snow.

She was in there deep. REALLY DEEP.

I had tripped her.

And how does a pile of snow trip somebody? You see, after everything that had happened: after turning into a shark, helping a group of Mopes battle Zeds in an underground world, turning into volcanic ash, surviving a variety of predatory birds, and then falling back to the ground—after everything that had happened—I may have been just a clump of wet snow.....

And apparently, so did my principal. After Pomperdash extracted herself from the snow, she balled her fists at her sides and shouted a few of those words we're not allowed to use at school. Then she yelled "STUPID SNOW" and she cocked back her foot and kicked me with everything she had. I went flying through the air and was headed directly for the windshield of a car. I crashed into that windshield and came face-to-face with the driver.

The woman at first didn't pay me any attention which was weird since this woman was MY MOTHER! Then, like a switch flipped, my mom's eyes about popped out of her head, she screamed, the car violently stopped and I rolled off the hood of the car and landed on the ground.

HARD.

IT HURT.

Landing on the ground as volcanic ash hadn't hurt. Landing on the ground as fluffy white snow hadn't hurt either. But falling a few feet from the hood of my mom's car had hurt. A lot.

I laid there for a long moment before I heard more familiar voices.

"Eddie, is that you?" David said as he stood over me.

"Honey, you're alive?" screamed my mom. "You're not a shark! You're a boy!"

Mom picked me up and gave me a hug and I hugged her back. That's when it hit me. I really was a boy. I had hands, a face, a torso, legs, knees, a back and well, of course, after everything I had been through...

I STILL HAD FEET.

"DUDE!" David said as he punched me in the shoulder.

"But you turned into a shark," he said. "Then we heard the helicopter had problems and you fell into the ocean. We thought you were a goner for sure. What happened?"

"It's kind of a long story."

"Well you can tell me tomorrow while we're sledding."

"We're sledding after school tomorrow?"

David smiled and then shook his head. "No dude, we're sledding INSTEAD of school tomorrow. I just heard Pomperdash. She said she was calling off school for the rest of the week."

I could hardly believe what I was hearing.

"She...she's calling off SCHOOL?"

"Yep."

"For the rest of the WEEK?"

"Incredible, right?"

"Was it because of what happened to me? I bet the whole school was pretty sad about it."

"Not so much, man. This IS Pomperdash we're talking about. No, she slipped on some ice a couple minutes ago. You totally missed it. Epic. She fell face first into a snow drift and I saw it. Amazing. Hey, you don't think you're gonna turn into a shark again do you?"

"She really called off school?" I asked.

"Yeah bro," David squinted and craned his neck toward me. He pointed his finger at my mouth. "You still got that shark tooth in your mouth."

I'd almost forgotten. I reached into my mouth, and sure enough the shark tooth was still there, wedged in that gap where my old tooth had been. I grabbed hold and yanked.

The shark tooth popped right out and I threw it as far as I could. It landed in the middle of the street. And that's the last I saw of it. Mom took me home, made me my favorite meal, and David and I spent the rest of the week making snow forts and sledding. It was the best week of my childhood.

And to think, it all started because of a loose tooth.

There was a long pause, and Rachel put her face inches from the door.

"And that's it, Grandpa?"

That's quite a bit, don't you think?

"Yeah," Rachel said. *"I do. I really do."*

The door clicked and opened and Rachel

stood there, her mouth open in a big broad smile. Except,

something was missing.

"Your tooth!" Grandpa exclaimed. "It came out!"

Rachel held her hand out and sure enough the tooth lay in her

palm.

"It didn't come out. I pulled it. And you were right, it didn't

hurt at all. Well, it hurt a little. But I've heard Mom play the violin too. It hurt way less than that."

"I'm proud of you Granddaughter."

"I'm glad mom called you and I'm glad you came over. That story really helped."

"I don't know what you're talking about. Your mother never called me."

"For real?" said Rachel.

"For real. I really did come over to tell you something."

"You did? What?"

"Well, you've been so preoccupied with that tooth, I don't think you took the time to look outside. Because if you had, you'd have noticed we got ourselves a nice little snow last night. School got called off for the day."

Rachel's eyes got big. "It did?"

"Indeed. And I thought, with a whole day of nothing to do, maybe you'd join me for a day at the museum."

"THE MUSEUM!"

"And especially now that you've lost your first tooth, I'd say it's the fitting way to celebrate. And maybe, if you play your cards right, maybe we'll make it to *Otto's* for a milkshake."

"Grandpa, you're the best."

"Tell me something I don't know. In fact, I suppose we don't even need to take the subway today. I could call us a cab, get us there more quickly."

Rachel's smile relaxed just a little and she moved her eyes around like she was thinking about something.

"Grandpa, do you think it would be okay if we walked today?"

"Walk? In all this snow?"

"Yes," said Rachel.

"You're sure?"

"Yes Grandpa, I'm sure. Because even though I lost my tooth today, you know what?"

"What?"

"I STILL HAVE FEET."

Grandpa put his hands in his pockets, curled his bottom lip over his top, leaned back and HMMMMMMMMED. He shook his head and laughed. "You're a very smart girl you know that, Granddaughter?"

Rachel laughed. "And Grandpa, you don't suppose you could tell me another story on our walk, do you?"

"Another story? Hmmm, well, let me think. Have I ever told you about the time I wrestled the two-headed crocodile?

"No Grandpa, you haven't.

"Then put on your boots, we've got a long walk ahead of us."

THE END

WANT TO GET A FREE STORY FROM ME?

If you are a parent and would like to sign up for my newsletter to get information about new releases, sales, AND free stories, please visit my website www.DanielKenney.com. You will immediately gain access to FREE stories.

Thanks so much for reading!

Daniel Kenney

CAN YOU HELP ME WITH A REVIEW?

Can you help me spread the word about BUT, I STILL HAD FEET? If you enjoyed reading, I would be honored if you asked a parent to help you write a short review about my book on Amazon.com. Those honest reviews really help readers find my books, and I want to introduce this silly story to as many readers as possible. Thank you so much for your help!

OTHER BOOKS BY
DANIEL KENNEY

The Beef Jerky Gang

Curial Diggs And The Search For The Romanov Dolls

Dart Guns At Dawn

Lunchmeat Lenny 6th Grade Crime Boss

Middle Squad

The Math Inspectors 1

The Math Inspectors 2

The Big Life of Remi Muldoon

Tales Of A Pirate Ninja

Visit DanielKenney.com where parents can sign up to receive

his newsletter and a free story.

DANIEL KENNEY

Visit DanielKenney.com to learn

how you could get a FREE story.

ABOUT THE AUTHOR
DANIEL KENNEY

Daniel Kenney and his wife Teresa live in Omaha, Nebraska with zero cats, zero dogs, one gecko and lots of kids. When those kids aren't driving him nuts, Daniel is busy writing books, cheering on the Benedictine Ravens, and plotting to take over the world. Daniel is the co-author of the Amazon Bestselling Detective series, The Math Inspectors. He is also the author of The Beef Jerky Gang, Middle Squad, Tales of a Pirate Ninja, The Big Life of Remi Muldoon, Curial Diggs World Treasure Hunter and other smart and funny books for kids. To learn more, please go to www.DanielKenney.com where parents will be able sign up for a FREE story.

Made in the USA
San Bernardino, CA
26 November 2016